YOGA
for School Children

BIJOYLAXMI HOTA

Rupa & Co

Text Copyright © Bijoylaxmi Hota 2008
Design Copyright © Rupa & Co. 2008

First Published 2008
Second Impression 2010

Published by
Rupa Publications India Pvt. Ltd.
7/16, Ansari Road, Daryaganj
New Delhi 110 002

Sales Centres:

Allahabad Bengaluru Chandigarh Chennai
Hyderabad Jaipur Kathmandu
Kolkata Mumbai

All rights reserved.
No part of this publication may be reproduced, stored in
a retrieval system, or transmitted, in any form or by any
means, electronic, mechanical, photocopying, recording or
otherwise, without the prior permission of the publishers.

Photographs
Rahul Dutta

Models
For cover: Vinitha Menon and Ria Dutt
For inside pages: Baduli Jain and others

Make-up
Meenakshi Dutt

Designed and illustrated by Ishtihaar

Printed in India by
Nutech Photolithographers
B-240, Okhla Industrial Area, Phase-I,
New Delhi 110 020, India

With the blessings of my Guru and Guide

Paramahamsa Swami Satyananda Saraswati

Contents

HEALTHY BODY AND SOUND MIND	8
ACNE	14
ANGER	26
ASTHMA	32
COMMON COLD	44
DYSMENORRHEA	52
OBESITY	68
SMOKING	84
STRESS AILMENTS	94
URINARY TRACT & DIGESTIVE TRACT INFECTION	106
MEDITATION	114
YOGANIDRA	120
HEALTH FACTS	126

CHAPTER 1

Healthy Body and Sound Mind

HEALTHY BODY AND SOUND MIND

What can be more distressing than seeing one's own children suffer due to ill health? And they seem to be falling sick all the time. While in school, they come in close contact with a large number of children; if one child is infected with a contagious disease, be it cough, flu, mumps or conjunctivitis, almost everybody else follows suit. By the time one disease subsides, another surfaces, claiming as many victims; and the crisis continues.

Infections are not the only cause of diseases in children. Stress is a major factor too. In one study, twelve per cent of the students of a school were found to have high blood pressure – the most visible effect of stress. Other common problems in children that may originate from this evil are asthma, stammering, bed-wetting and irritable bowel syndrome.

Another cause of ailments in children is environmental pollutants that get into a child's system in various ways. The water they drink contains forty different harmful chemicals, the food they eat is full of preservatives, colours, and pesticide residues; and the air they breathe has many poisonous gases and impurities. Though the liver is empowered to eliminate all unwanted elements from the system, it cannot do the job effectively when there are too many pollutants to handle. The excess toxins find their way into the body cells and slowly poison the tissues making them weak and diseased. Cancer is thought to be the outcome of excessive toxins and tension in the system. Almost all cancer patients are found to have a weak liver and a study revealed

that most of them had a series of traumatic experiences six to eighteen months prior to the onset of the disease.

Conventional therapy uses powerful antibiotics and other drugs to treat diseases. There is no doubt that they provide immediate relief, but they eventually end up harming the system, because these are chemical drugs that add to the existing toxins, making a body's internal environment more poisonous. As a result, the immune system becomes weak making the body susceptible to hordes of infections. Sometimes the drugs may not work at all as the microbes develop resistance to them. Many a death has occurred due to an infection contracted in a hospital where the microbes that are exposed to various drugs develop immunity. Furthermore, in conventional therapy, only the symptoms are alleviated, not the cause. For example, in hypothyroidism, where the thyroid gland secretes insufficient thyroxin leading to slow metabolism that results in various problems including obesity, this hormone is administered to fill up the deficiency; but nothing is done to normalise the functioning of the thyroid gland. The gland becomes progressively weaker and modern science has no means to strengthen it.

Yoga on the other hand, is a time-tested science that aims at rejuvenating all the glands and organs in the body ensuring their efficient functioning. It makes the immune system robust and a strong immune system can ward off all infections. In the past, when there were no effective drugs for diseases like plague, cholera and T.B.,

HEALTHY BODY AND SOUND MIND • 11

millions of people died, but millions also survived despite being exposed to the same microbes. It was only because their immune system fought the invaders and won. An efficient immune system can also detect and devour abnormal body cells which may have turned cancerous at a later stage.

Strong immune cells devour all invaders and potential cancer cells

To attain and maintain perfect physical and mental health, yoga has various techniques such as *asanas*, *pranayama*, *shatkarma* (cleansing techniques), meditation and *yoganidra*, i.e. yogic sleep. *Asanas* are of two types, dynamic and static. The dynamic *asanas* speed up blood circulation, exercise muscles and squeeze stored toxins out of the body tissues for *shatkarmas* to wash them out. Static *asanas*, on the other hand, carry more blood and *prana* (the vital bio-current) to target areas to heal and energise weak body parts. Simultaneously, stress is eliminated from the mind through meditation, *yoganidra*, music and chants. Specific techniques affect specific body parts and must be chosen carefully to attain the desired result. For example, a child with a family history of diabetes needs to include practices that strengthen the pancreas, while, children of heart patients must include those that are meant for the heart, to avoid acquiring these hereditary diseases in the future. But *Suryanamaskar* and *Nadisodhan pranayama* are the most essential yogic practices that should be included in all yogic routines.

Suryanamaskar is a dynamic practice incorporating seven different *asanas* to stretch, flex and massage all the body parts internal and external rendering them healthy and strong. Its effect is said to reach the tiniest of nerves, the thinnest of capillaries and the deepest of cells in the bones. An added advantage of this *asana* is that one can practice it for 108 rounds i.e. 216 times, to feel well exercised.

Nadisodhan pranayama, a breathing technique, literally means 'clearing the energy pathways'. Yoga holds that as long as *prana*, the vital force, flows smoothly in the energy channels called *nadis*, good health prevails. But these *nadis* get blocked due to excessive mental work and abuse of the body and as a result, there is a pooling of *prana* at some places, while some others go without it. This uneven distribution leads to low energy and illnesses. *Nadisodhan pranayama* as the name suggests, does the job of cleaning these blockages.

An appropriate yogic routine followed correctly and sincerely from childhood can not only cure and prevent ailments, but will also ensure proper physical and mental growth of the child. With a sound body and mind, children are bound to grow up to be more energetic, productive and innovative adults with a sunny disposition and a positive attitude towards life. Former British Prime Minister Tony Blair's idea of curbing terrorism by guiding children appropriately, right from the embryonic stage, may be a little impractical, but it is certainly not as ridiculous as it is being made out to be. According to yoga, if a pregnant woman is able to positively mould her body, mind

HEALTHY BODY AND SOUND MIND • 13

and psyche, its effect on the womb is total. Serious yoga practitioners are sure to become brilliant, but not cunning or cheats; they may become fiercely competitive, but not greedy enough to harm their rivals; and they may become overtly ambitious, but not cruel enough to take lives.

CHAPTER 2

Acne

ACNE

A child's smooth glowing skin is a gift of nature. But as children step into adolescence, most of them get afflicted with ugly acne. Acne as a term is used for a variety of skin eruptions such as blackheads, whiteheads, pimples and big boil-like lesions known as nodules. The former two conditions and a few pimples can be considered as mild manifestations of acne, while lots of large and painful nodules appearing on the face, chest and back are considered severe. In this condition, the nodules leave permanent scars on the skin.

Hormonal changes during puberty are the main cause of acne. Androgen hormones that cause physical maturation also stimulate the sebaceous glands to grow larger and secrete more sebum or oil. The glands are located in the sebaceous follicles of the hair shaft of the skin. The oil produced by them moves up through the shaft to the surface and is used to lubricate the skin. During puberty when everything speeds up, the cells of the follicle are also shed rapidly. These cells stick together and plug the opening of the shaft and the sebum finds no way to escape, accumulating in the follicles and making them swell up. The stagnant white sebum that is seen under the skin is called a white head. When the excessive pressure of the sebum forces open the skin, exposing the substance which then attracts dirt and turns black, it is known as a black head. Sometimes, the exposed grime gives rise to bacterial breeding leading to inflammation and pus formation and resulting in pimples. In extreme conditions, large and painful nodules are formed.

Acne generally subsides once a teenager steps into adulthood, but in some cases, it persists even into the thirties. Acne may not be a health hazard, but the sight of patchy, unbecoming skin can be quite daunting for a young mind, leading to various psychological problems. Children may become shy, self-conscious and low on self esteem. Sometimes the problem can be very deep and scar their psyche permanently.

Yogic remedy for acne is simple but should be used as a preventive, not as a curative measure, because once the skin acquires deep scars and open pores, yoga can do precious little to rectify the condition. Meditation and *asanas* such as *Kandhrasana* normalise the overactive sebaceous gland decreasing oil production, while *Suryanamaskar* generates the necessary heat in the skin to melt and evacuate the stagnant sebum from the shaft.

TECHNIQUE

Suryanamaskar

Step 1. Stand straight with hands folded in front of the chest.

Step 2. Inhaling, raise your arms and stretch as far back as possible.

18 • YOGA FOR SCHOOL CHILDREN

Step 3. Exhaling, bend forward and place your hands on the floor in front and outside of your feet. (Try not to bend the legs).

Step 4. Inhaling, extend the right leg back and lower the hips with the head held back.

Step 5. Exhaling, take the left leg back to join the feet, while lifting the hips up to form a triangle with your trunk.

ACNE • 19

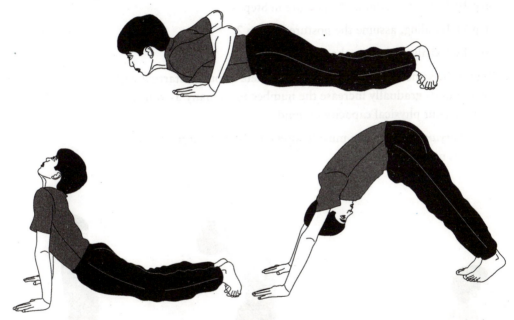

Step 6. Holding your breath, lower your body to the floor. Only the hips should not touch the floor.

Step 7. Drop the hips, then inhaling, raise your trunk with the head held back.

Step 8. Exhaling, assume the posture in Step 5

Step 9. Inhaling, assume the posture in Step 4

20 • YOGA FOR SCHOOL CHILDREN

Step 10. Exhaling, assume the posture in Step 3

Step 11. Inhaling, assume the posture in Step 2

Step 12. Exhaling, assume the posture in Step 1

Repeat the same on the other side to complete a round. Starting with three rounds gradually increase the number to as many as you want keeping your physical capacity in mind.

After *Suryanamaskar*, one must lie down in *Shavasana* till breathing becomes normal.

ACNE • **21**

Pranamasana

- Sit in *Vajrasana*
- Hold your calves
- Exhaling, bend forward and place the forehead on the ground. Holding the breath raise your hips while rolling the head to rest on the corner (where Hindus keep their tuft).
- Breathe normally for a few seconds, inhaling sit up and exhale.
- Lie down in *Shavasana* for half a minute. Gradually increase the duration of the final posture to one minute.

Dhanurasana

- Lie down on your stomach, bend the legs and hold the ankles.
- Inhale and raise your head and legs to resemble a bow.
- Hold the posture for a few seconds.
- Exhaling, return to the starting posture. Repeat three times. The duration of the final posture should be increased to as long as you can hold your breath comfortably.

Halasana

- Lie down with the legs together.
- Inhale and lift legs up and keeping them straight, take them towards the floor, away from the head.
- Breathe normally for a few seconds.
- Inhale and holding the breath in, return to the starting position.
- Rest till breathing is normal.

Nadisodhan Pranayama

- Sit in *Padmasana* or *Sukhasana* (crossed legged).
- Touch the base of your left thumb with the tip of your index finger.
- Keep the left hand on the left knee.
- Place the index and middle fingers of the right hand in between the eyebrows.
- Maintain a straight posture.
- Close the right nostril with your thumb and breathe deeply from the left one.
- Close the left nostril with the ring finger and breathe out from the right one.
- Practice in the reverse to complete one round.
- Repeat the round ten times.

It must be remembered that too much heat in the form of steam may unplug and clear the shaft, but it can also enlarge the pores. Instead, gram flour should be used to clean the skin and soak up the oil. A mild soap may be used to clean the skin, but the face should not be washed more than two to three times a day as it can rob the skin off all its natural lubricant and make it dry, flaky and irritable. Application of turmeric and sandalwood paste is extremely beneficial as the former is a powerful antiseptic and anti-bacterial while the latter is soothing and rejuvenating.

Gram flour applied as a facial mask, soaks up oil from the skin

CHAPTER 3

Anger

ANGER

A nger is a corroding emotion that creates havoc in the system. Sudden and intense anger can lead to a heart attack resulting in death. Rage can arrest the digestive processes, ceasing them completely. An experiment on an enraged dog showed that no digestive juices were secreted in his body even hours after it had calmed down. Another study revealed how a man's stomach shed its lining and became red and raw every time he got angry. Eating in such conditions not only strains the system, but also causes improper digestion. This in turn, leads to malnourishment and weakening of the entire body, clearing the path for ill health.

The appearance of an angry person is also affected adversely. During a burst of anger, the facial features change drastically. The eyes become big and blood shot; the lips tighten to a thin line; nostrils flare up and the jaw becomes taut. The face regains its original contours only after the rage passes. But if it happens once too often, the facial muscles may not be able to return to their normal position properly, retaining some tension permanently and changing one's appearance to that of perpetual anger. No wonder it is said that the face mirrors the inner self.

Angry people suffer in several other ways too. They can hardly make lasting friends; even close relatives start avoiding them. Thus, ostracised by their near and dear ones, they may lead a lonely and miserable life, not knowing what to do about it.

Yoga is one of the best ways to change the situation, as it helps control anger to a great extent. Since anger is caused due to the over-secretion of adrenal hormones, *asanas* that control this gland are a great help. Also, the stress hormones released into the blood stream due to anger, which need to be used up to protect the system from harm, is achieved through dynamic *asanas* while *Pranayama* successfully calms the nerves and the mind. Meditation helps in further control of the mind. Repetition of words which are the antonym of the word 'anger' such as *shanti,* 'peace', 'calm' or 'cool' are also extremely effective.

Aniruddh, another of my students, whom I treated for stress with yoga and meditation writes – "At the time I began my classes with Mrs. Hota my blood pressure was 160/100. Furthermore, I felt very stressed which often caused me to be irritable and aggressive. Within three classes, my blood pressure fell to 140/90. I began to feel less aggressive and irritable and felt an overall sense of inner tranquility."

The most beneficial *asana* to control one's anger is *Shashankasana*.

ANGER • 29

TECHNIQUE

Shashankasana

- Sit in *Vajrasana*
- Inhaling, raise your arms.
- Exhaling, bend forward and keep the forehead and forearms on the ground.
- Breathe normally.

The duration of the *asana* can be determined according to the intensity of one's anger. People with long, intense bouts of rage can do it for as long as half an hour. For children, five minutes is normally sufficient.

Other helpful practices:

Sambhavi Mudra

- Sit straight in any meditative posture such as *Vajrasana*.
- Close your eyes.
- Relax the body.
- Open your eyes and look up.
- Focus your gaze on the point between the eyebrows. In the correct position, this part forms a wide-angled 'V'.
- Gaze at the tip of the angle for a few seconds, and then close the eyes.
- Repeat three rounds.

Bhoochari Mudra

- Sit straight in *Padmasana* with the left hand on the left knee in *Gyana Mudra*.
- Close your eyes and relax.
- Open your eyes and lift the right hand to the face with the palm down and the elbow out.
- Placing the thumbnail under the nose, gaze at the tip of the little finger without blinking.

- After a minute, remove the hand but still gaze at the same point for as long as you can.
- Continue practicing this for four to five minutes.
- Breathing should be natural.

Paschimottanasana

- Sit down with the legs extended in front.
- Inhaling, raise your arms.
- Exhaling, bend forward and try to hold the toes without bending your legs.
- Keep your head down.
- Breathe normally.
- Starting with five breaths, gradually increase the number to twenty.

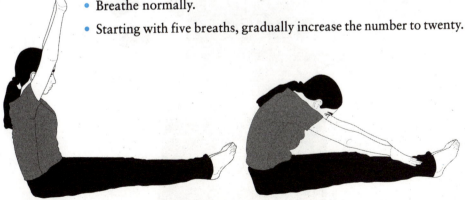

CHAPTER 4

Asthma

ASTHMA

Asthma is a leading cause of chronic illness in children today. Up to ten per cent of children suffer from this ailment, most of them from before the age of ten. Though death caused due to asthma is rare, asthma can be a distressing and debilitating disease. It is not easy for a child to fight for every breath, which is what happens during an asthmatic attack. The attack generally starts with a cold and cough accompanied by excessive mucus production. Soon the lining in the airways swells up, narrowing down the passage. This, along with the presence of mucus, makes it extremely difficult for air to pass through. The amount of air the child manages to inhale is therefore quite inadequate. To meet the body's demand for oxygen, the heart beats faster, sometimes dangerously so, needing emergency medical treatment. The attack may last for a few minutes or a few days, leaving the child completely drained.

Asthma leaves its marks on the body and mind of its victims. It stunts their physical growth, creates fear and stress in them and restricts their activities. Such children are advised to stay away from all irritants such as smoke, dust, animals, certain kinds of food and everything that is cold.

Medical science is yet to discover what causes asthma, labelling it an allergy that is triggered by factors ranging from pollen and mold spores to exercise and anti-inflammatory drugs including aspirin. It treats the ailment with anti-allergens, bronchodilators and steroids, all of which are harmful in the long run. They can harden the lungs and destroy brain cells. Yogic treatment on the other hand, is safe and effective.

Kshitij came to me when he was six or seven years old. Like most asthmatics, he was a thin, narrow-chested and restless child with very poor concentration. I barely managed to teach him the necessary yogic techniques and wrote down a strict diet. He did not give me the impression that he would follow them properly. But a year later when I saw him, I was pleasantly surprised. The child had transformed into a robust, reasonable and energetic boy who had suffered no asthmatic attack from the very first day of his yoga practice. I invited him and his mother to the television programme on yoga I was making at that time, to show and tell the viewers about the simple *asana* that cured him. Yoga regards asthma as a psychosomatic disorder that is caused by a traumatic experience in early childhood and treats it accordingly. Along with meditation to remove the negative impression, *asanas* and *Pranayama* that broaden the chest and strengthen the respiratory organs are practiced. At the same time, excess mucus is removed from the body by *Shatkarma* such as *Kunjal* (vomiting).

Anti-asthmatic spray destroys the brain cells

Unfortunately, children younger than seven

years of age cannot practice the necessary techniques. But sometimes, simple practices such as *Makarasana* and *Shashankasan* which are easy for a child to perform, along with induced vomiting help. For this, the *asanas* should be performed everyday and at the first sign of a cold or cough, the child should be made to drink a glass of warm, saline water. Ideally, the child should vomit it out, but failing to do so is not harmful as the salt water will dissolve the excess mucus and eliminate it from the system.

Basil plants can sometimes do wonders. A one-year-old who was diagnosed with asthma never suffered a second attack after I tried a few simple tricks. First, on my advice, she was kept surrounded by basil plants. Even when she traveled in a car, two or three pots of basil were kept near her. Simultaneously, I used to touch her body parts lightly on the principles of *Yoganidra* and at the end whisper into her ears a suggestion to overcome the ailment, which was repeated again during her sleep. Perhaps the combination worked.

Basil helps in cure of asthma

36 • YOGA FOR SCHOOL CHILDREN

The following is the complete routine for older asthmatic children.

Hasta Utthanasana

- Stand with your legs apart and your hands in front, crossed at the wrists.
- Inhaling, raise your arms, maintaining the position of the hands.
- Turn your face up to look at the hands.
- Exhaling, bring your arms down to the sides.
- Inhaling, lift them up from the sides and cross the wrists again above you.
- Exhaling, return your hands to the starting position.
- Repeat the *asana* ten times.

ASTHMA • 37

Hasta Uttahanasana II

- Stand straight with your feet apart and hands folded in front.
- Inhaling, push your hands forward and then spread the arms out taking them as far back as possible.
- Exhaling, bring your arms back to the sides.
- Repeat the *asana* ten times.

Ushtrasana

- Stand on your knees.
- Separate the knees to be in line with the shoulders.
- Bend backwards and hold your ankles.
- Your head should be bent as far back as possible without any tension.
- Hold the posture for a few seconds and return to the starting position.
- Gradually increase the duration and breathe naturally for a minute or two.

Sarvangasana

- Lie down on your back on the floor.
- Placing your hands under your back, lift your body into a vertical position.
- The head and shoulder should remain on the ground with the trunk touching the chin.
- Breathe normally.
- Starting with five or ten breaths, gradually increase to forty or fifty.

Matsyasana

(To be practiced for half the duration of *Sarvangasana*)

- Sit in *Padmasana*.
- Bend backwards
- Supporting the body with your hands and arching the back, lower the corner of your head to the ground.
- Hold your toes
- Breathe naturally

The durations of *Sarvangasana* and *Matsyasana* should always be in the ratio 2: 1

Lolasana

- Sit in *Padmasana* with your hands on the floor at the sides.
- Take a deep breath and lift up your body.
- Hold the posture for as long as you can.
- Exhaling, lower your body.

42 • YOGA FOR SCHOOL CHILDREN

Makarasana

- Lie down on your stomach.
- Prop your body up with your hands under the chin.
- Your forearms should be vertical to the ground.
- Breathe normally.

Starting with five breaths, gradually increase the count to 100.

Bhastrika Pranayama

- Assume the posture in *Nadisodhan Pranayama* and breathe forcefully twenty times from the left nostril, twenty times from the right and then removing your hand from your face twenty times from both.

This is one round.

Practice one round in the summer and three to five rounds in winter.

CHAPTER 5

Common Cold

COMMON COLD

One of the most frequent illnesses that children suffer from is common cold, an infection caused by as many as two hundred different viral strains and transmitted through respiratory tract secretions. A cold can be a very uncomfortable experience what with a stuffy nose, sore throat, watery eyes, heavy head, headache and body ache. Though common cold is considered a minor ailment that subsides on its own in a few days, at times it can lead to serious bacterial infections of the ears, throat and lungs needing aggressive medical treatment with antibiotics. Unfortunately, what most people don't know is that repeated attacks of cold and cough in children can prove to be quite dangerous. Chronic cold can lead to adenoid growth that blocks the nasal passage forcing a child to breathe from the mouth. And perpetual breathing through the mouth is extremely harmful because a lack of intellectual ability has been noticed in children who breathe in this manner. I have myself come across a few such children whose I.Q. was so low and their grasp was so poor that they could not learn any of the yogic exercises I tried to teach them, which is why I have no idea if yoga could have reversed their condition.

Even in its milder form, breathing through the mouth is detrimental to health, because unlike the nasal passage, the mouth cannot filter the dirt and pollutants which enter the body with the air we breathe. The hair in the nose remove suspended particles while the mucus secreted in the nasal passage traps the smaller particles that escape filtering. At the same time, the huge numbers of blood vessels contained in the nose warm the air bringing it to one's body temperature. Untreated air can cause extensive damage to the delicate lung tissue. Damaged lungs cannot provide the required amount of oxygen needed by the body tissues, causing them to become weak and ailing. Common cold should be contained early in life to relieve the child of such misery and also to prevent unpleasant consequences.

Though children are administered antibiotics at times, these drugs have no effect on viruses. Decongestants, cough syrups and cough drops may help to relieve some symptoms, but they neither cure the ailment nor shorten its duration. On top of that, they can lead to stomach problems. Nasal sprays too help only temporarily and their continuous use can cause greater congestion in the nose in between applications calling for progressively higher and more frequent dosage.

Yogic *Shatkarma*, *Kunjal* and *Neti*, done at the first sign of an approaching cold, along with proper care, control the ailment effectively. Salt water, not only removes mucus from the nose, it also kills the infection. A proper diet is recommended to further aid healing. Since over-eating, over-activity, exposure to cold, rich food and mucus producing foods such as milk products, rice, banana and white flour worsen cold, they should be avoided. The afflicted child should drink a lot of hot fluids like soup and rest in a warm

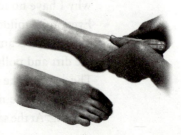

Massaging feet with mustard oil and garlic increases the inner body temperature and combats cold.

room with the chest and upper arms covered. Massaging the soles twice a day with warm mustard oil heated with garlic and caraway seeds is extremely beneficial. Drinking a decoction of basil, ginger and bay leaf sweetened with honey is soothing and helps fight cold effectively. But one should aim at strengthening the child's immune system through the following yogic *asanas*.

Simhasana

- Sit in *Vajrasana* and move the knees wide apart.
- Place your hands on the floor in between the knees with the fingers pointing inward.
- Throw your head back.
- Look at the 'V' point in between the eyebrows.
- Take a deep breath.
- Open your mouth wide
- Stick your tongue out.
- Exhale from the mouth with an aaaaaah..... sound

Repeat the *asana* ten times.

Dwikonasana

- Stand straight with your hands clasped at the back.
- Inhale.
- Exhaling, bend forward while lifting your arms up.
- Inhaling, return to the starting position.

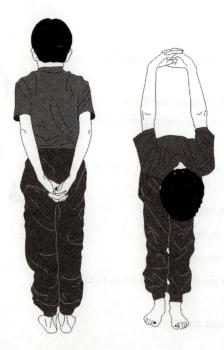

COMMON COLD • **49**

Shankukhi Mudra

- Sit in *Padmasana*.
- Plug your ears with your thumbs.
- Place the index fingers on closed eyes and close your nostrils with the middle fingers. Keep the ring fingers under the nose and the little fingers under the lips.
- Remove the middle fingers and breathe deeply. Close and hold your breath for as long as you can.

Continue the *asana* for two to three minutes.

50 • YOGA FOR SCHOOL CHILDREN

Neti

- Fill the *Neti* pot with warm saline water.
- The water should be slightly warmer than your body temperature and as salty as a tear.
- Insert the spout into your left nostril blocking it completely.
- Breathe from the mouth throughout the practice.
- Bend forward.
- Bend your head to the right while lifting the pot.
- The water will flow out of the right nostril. When the pot is empty, remove it, still breathing from the mouth.
- (The pot can be removed anytime, but continue breathing through the mouth).
- Blow your nose.
- Repeat the exercise from the other side.
- Bend forward for half a minute with your hands held behind.
- Water will drip out.
- Straighten up and bend your head back.
- Blow your nose to make sure no water is left in the nose.

- Assume the final posture of *Shashankasana* and remain in that position for one minute and breathe from the mouth.
- Practise *Kapalabhati pranayama* to dry the nostrils.

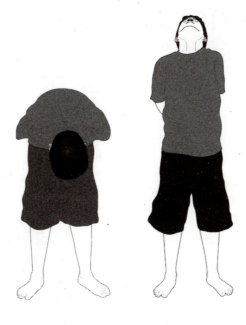

The nose must be cleared with *Neti* whenever it is blocked and adenoid growth must be prevented for which *Shankukhi Mudra* is very effective.

Chapter 6

Dysmenorrhea

DYSMENORRHEA

Recently I was visiting a relative when her fourteen-year-old daughter phoned her from school asking to be brought back home immediately. She was experiencing excruciating period pain in spite of taking two painkillers. I was aghast. At such a young age she had to consume such high dosages of this medicine, which is known to cause pinprick bleeding in the stomach even in the smallest dose, which in turn can lead to digestive disorders such as acidity and irritable bowel syndrome. The mother was fully aware of the risks, but was helpless because of her daughter's present agony. Period pain or dysmenorrhea is a common problem faced by more than half the girls, with at least ten per cent of them suffering more severely than the others. The pain is felt mostly in the lower abdomen, but may also extend to the hips, lower back and thighs. Sometimes it is accompanied by nausea, vomiting, diarrhea and body ache.

Excessive levels of prostaglandin substances that make the uterus contract during child birth are thought to be the cause of simple dysmenorrhea. Though certain gynaecological disorders can also lead to period pain, such cases are very rare. Dysmenorrhea is not a serious problem and generally disappears after the birth of the first child, but it can make a young girl's life miserable.

Medically, the only answer to dysmenorrhea is gulping down an analgesic. Initially a mild dose can provide relief, but after a while it becomes ineffective calling for progressively higher dosage which slowly poisons the girl's system, exposing her to various health problems.

Yoga on the other hand provides relief sans any risk. It first aims to normalise the functioning of the pituitary gland by providing it with more blood and energy. Only a healthy pituitary gland can regulate the functions of all other glands, including the ones that govern the female reproductive cycles, correctly. Yoga also improves the health of the ovaries ensuring controlled secretion of the offending hormones.

Food plays a very important role in managing period pain. In many girls, acidic fruits and vegetables such as lemon, orange, tomato and curd immediately increase the pain. These girls should abstain from all such items for a week prior and during their period. Some girls also develop acute hyperacidity that gives them gastric pain as excruciating as the cramps in the uterus. These girls should eliminate not only acidic food items, but also stay away from all acid producing ones such as coffee, beans, black gram, red chili, white flour, rich spicy food and animal products, mainly meat, fish, chicken and cheese during and prior to the onset of the monthly cycle. They should have brown bread, lentil soup, and boiled or steamed vegetables. Certain vegetables like cauliflower, cabbage and radish produce gas and should be avoided. In extreme cases only gourds i.e. bottle, ridge and lined, should be taken.

Gulkand, a rose confection, is an excellent natural antacid and it can be taken after meals and whenever the need arises.

School-going girls with time constraints may find the yogic routine

too lengthy. They can start with only three or four *asanas* and go on adding to the list as and when necessary. I taught only *Suryanamaskar*, *Marjari* and *Kandhrasana* to the above mentioned girl and she called me up to say that she needed only one painkiller during her next monthly period. One may also divide the routine into three segments and practice one segment a day.

Acidic fruits and vegetables like lemon, oranges and tomatoes as well as acid producing foods like coffee and red chillies should be avoided during periods

The complete yogic routine
TECHNIQUE

Marjari Asana

- Sit in Vajrasana.
- Measure one forearm and one hand length from your knees and place your hands such that when you rise to your all fours, your arms are vertical.
- Move your hands apart to bring them just under the shoulders.
- Inhaling, bend your head as far back as you comfortably can, while depressing your back.
- Exhaling, bend your head forward as you arch your back.

The movement is similar to the stretching of a cat. Repeat the *asana* ten times

Kandhrasana

- Lie down on your back.
- Bend your legs and place your feet flat near the hips.
- Hold your ankles
- Inhale and lift your pelvis up. Hold the posture for as long as comfortable.
- Exhaling return to the starting position.
- Repeat three times.

58 • YOGA FOR SCHOOL CHILDREN

Sarvangasana

- Lie down on your back on the floor.
- Placing your hands under your back, lift your body into a vertical position.
- The head and shoulder should remain on the ground with the trunk touching the chin.
- Breathe normally.
- Starting with five or ten breaths, gradually increase to forty or fifty.

Dhanurasana

- Lie down on your stomach, bend the legs and hold the ankles.
- Inhale and raise your head and legs to resemble a bow.
- Hold the posture for a few seconds.
- Exhaling, return to the starting posture. Repeat three times. The duration of the final posture should be increased to as long as you can hold your breath comfortably.

60 • YOGA FOR SCHOOL CHILDREN

Chakki Chalana

- Sit down with your legs extended before you.
- Clasp your fingers and hold your hands near your abdomen.
- Exhaling and moving the hands clockwise to the feet, bend forward.
- Inhaling and still moving the hands clockwise to your abdomen bend backwards.

Repeat it clockwise ten times and then do it another ten times moving your hands anti-clockwise.

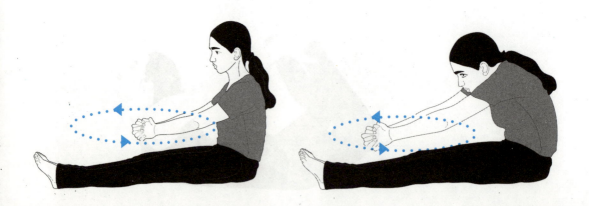

DYSMENORRHEA • 61

Naukasanchalana

The body movement in this asana is the same as in the previous one, only the hands move differently here.

- Close your hands into fists.
- Lift up your arms and move them down and forward in a circular pattern like rowing a boat. After doing this ten times, open your palms and starting from the sides of your thigh, move them forward and up, then back and down.

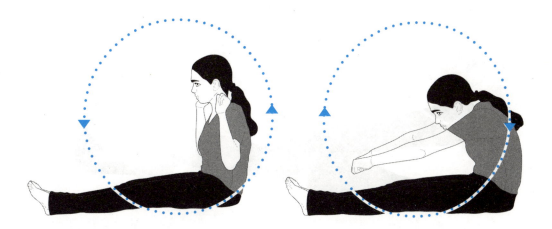

Leg Rotation

- Lie down on your back with your arms on the sides of the body.
- Lift the right leg and keeping it straight, rotate it clockwise five times and then anticlockwise five times.

Repeat the *asana* with the other leg.

DYSMENORRHEA • 63

Cycling

Remain in the position mentioned in the previous technique. Lift your legs up and reproduce the cycling movement.

Leg Pressing

- Remain in the position mentioned in the previous technique.
- Bend the right leg and bring the knee close to your chest.
- Interlock your fingers and fold the bent leg.
- Exhale.
- Lift your head to touch your knee with your nose while pressing the leg down to the chest.
- Hold the posture for as long as you feel comfortable.
- Inhaling, lower the head and relax your hold on the leg.
- After a brief rest, repeat the exercise.

Practise the *asana* five times with each leg.

Practise the same, holding both your legs together.

Tadagi Mudra

- Sit with your legs stretched in front with both hands on the legs.
- Lean forward and hold the big toe on each foot while keeping your head straight.
- Breathe ten times, slowly and deeply.
- Return to the starting position.

Practise the exercise two to three times.

Moola Bandha

- Sit in *Padmasana* with your hands on the knees.
- Take a deep breath.
- Exhaling through pursued lips, (it makes a hissing sound), bend your head forward and touch your chest with your chin.
- Lift your shoulders and straighten your arms to lock the posture.
- Contract the perineum.
- Hold the posture for as long as is comfortable.
- Release the perineum; release the shoulder lock, lift your head to the normal position and inhale.

Repeat it five times.

Shatkarma

The yogic cleansing technique *Kunjal* should be performed for four to five days prior to the onset of the monthly cycle to reduce acidity and gas formation.

Home remedies

One teaspoon of asafetida taken with warm water is very effective for period pain.

Half a cup of hot water with two spoons of honey gives instant relief from gas pain.

Marjari asana and the *Om* chant also help to relieve cramps.

Obesity

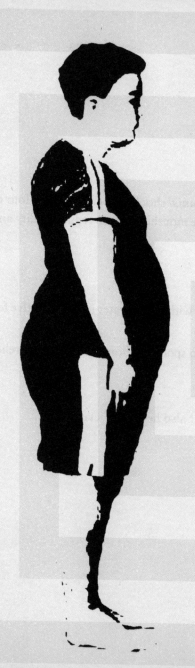

OBESITY

Obesity in children has become one of the greatest health concerns the world over although the situation is worse in developed countries. In the USA for instance, fifteen per cent of children between the ages of six to nine are overweight, and their number is on the rise.

Besides being uncomfortable, ungainly and demoralising, obesity is a serious health hazard with its prime victim being the heart. The chief cause of high blood pressure in twelve per cent of schoolchildren was obesity, a study revealed. This is because the heart needs to work harder to supply blood to the billions of extra tissues and the strain can exhaust this vital organ prematurely.

Obesity can also damage the liver. One out of every fifteen obese people is sure to suffer from a weak liver. First, fat accumulates in the liver and causes it to swell; gradually the liver cells begin to deteriorate and once eighty per cent of the organ has been damaged, water starts accumulating in the stomach, which has often proved to be fatal. What makes this problem difficult to detect is the fact that it displays no early symptoms and by the time the problem is discovered, it is usually too late. Other ailments linked to obesity are diabetes, gallbladder diseases, cancer, impotence and sleep apnea. To avoid falling prey to these diseases, obesity needs to be cured sooner than later.

Besides hereditary factors, it is the lifestyle that children lead today which is making them obese. They, like their elders, lead a sedentary life reading, writing, watching television, playing videogames and working on the computer; while the food they consume chips, pizzas, burgers, cakes and ice creams contain high amounts of calories. It is natural that when the calorie intake exceeds the body's need, the extra calories are converted to fat. What's more, these eatables are poor quality food devoid of any nutrition and may also lead to nutritional deficiencies and a disturbed metabolism.

Lack of calcium and iron can also lead to obesity.

Another theory suggests that since the body recognises only natural, wholesome food as real food, in its absence, the body may anticipate starvation and convert all available calories to fat, a reaction dating to man's primitive beginnings. The primitive people did not know where or when their next meal would come from and to preserve themselves during the lean phases, their bodies stored fat.

The metabolism of the body, that is the rate at which a body burns calories, is regulated by the thyroid gland. A healthy, active, thyroid burns many more calories than a sluggish one. This is the reason why some people remain slim despite an extremely high intake of food, while some go an adding weight though they eat very little.

Lack of calcium and iron can also lead to obesity

Fat melts when the body's demand for energy rises. Hence children need to increase their physical activities first. All kinds of physical exercises lead to the burning of calories, but yoga has an edge over other systems because it consists not only of dynamic exercises which increase the body's demand for energy, but also strikes at the core of the problem aiming to improve the health of the thyroid and speed up the metabolic rate. *Guru Shankha Prakshyalana* is a *Shatkarma* that is extremely effective in activating this gland. I have known people to lose as much as ten kilos in two weeks by just performing this *kriya* (practice). But it needs to be practiced under expert supervision and only older children, those above the age of thirteen, can do it.

Vipareet Karani Mudra and *Sarvangasan*a are also effective in improving the health of the thyroid gland while all dynamic *asanas* help burn calories faster.

Most weight loss programmes include drastic food restrictions. But children should never be made to starve or follow limiting dietary patterns. Not only can it hamper their growth and development, it also proves to be quite useless. According to an institute that is a part of the National Academy of Science in Washington D.C., people on diets may lose around one-tenth of their body weight after completing a weight loss programme, but generally gain two-thirds of it within a year and almost the entire weight within five years. Fad diets should also be avoided as they can cause irreversible damage to the system.

For example, a high protein, low carbohydrate diet leaves behind a lot of uric acid, the end product of all proteins, for the kidney to expel from the system which can put too much strain on these vital organs and cause renal problems.

Decreasing carbohydrate intake is also unwise since it has its own use. When the body has received sufficient amounts of carbohydrates, the craving for more food disappears. Besides, carbs burn faster and are not easily converted into fat. Complex carbohydrates such as fruits and vegetables are even better as they contain high amounts of fibre that soak up the fat, preventing it from getting absorbed into the blood stream.

All children need to do is to reduce their intake of pure fats such as oil, butter and cream and fatty food such as cheese and pork. One study showed that there was no difference in calorie intake between a group of obese men and an equal number of lean ones. But the former group took thirty-three per cent of their total calories from fat alone. An ideal combination however consists of fifty-five per cent carbohydrates, fifteen to twenty percent protein, five per cent fat and the rest as roughage. Cabbage and celery soup and aniseed decoction are said to help burn fat. A glass of hot water with two teaspoons of

Cabbage and celery soup with lots of aniseeds can burn unwanted body fat

honey and the juice of one lemon taken in the morning on an empty stomach is also said to burn fat.

TECHNIQUE

Trikonasana I

- Stand with your feet apart.
- Clasp your hands behind you.
- Inhale.
- Bend your left leg and exhaling bend forward to touch the left knee with your nose.
- Inhaling, straighten up.
- Do the same thing with your right leg.
- Repeat the *asana* ten times.

Trikonasana II

- Stand with your feet apart and your arms extended to the sides.
- Exhaling and bending the left leg, bend to the left side and touch your foot with your left hand while turning your face up to look at the ceiling.
- Bring the right arm down to a horizontal position.
- Inhaling, return to the starting position and repeat with the right side to complete a round.

Practise ten rounds.

Shashankabhujangasana

- Sit in *Vajrasana* and place your hands as in *Marjari*.
- Inhaling, slide forward and rise to *Bhujangasana*.
- Exhaling, return to *Shashankasana*.
- Move continuously ten times.
- Rest in *Shashankasana* for a minute.

76 • YOGA FOR SCHOOL CHILDREN

Shashankabhujangasana

Shashankabhujangasana

Dhanurasana

- Lie down on your stomach, bend the legs and hold the ankles.
- Inhale and raise your head and legs to resemble a bow.
- Hold the posture for a few seconds.
- Exhaling, return to the starting posture. Repeat three times. The duration of the final posture should be increased to as long as you can hold your breath comfortably.

Vipareet Karani Mudra

- Assume *Sarvangasana*, and then lower the hips a little so that your trunk makes a sixty degree angle with the floor. Your legs should be vertical.
- Breathe normally for three minutes (Count sixty breaths).
- Return to *Sarvangasana* for *Dritahalasana*.

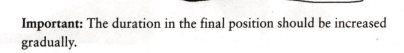

Important: The duration in the final position should be increased gradually.

Dritahalasana

- Assume *Sarvangasana*.
- Inhale and exhale.
- Take your legs back and down to touch the floor with your toes (the legs should not bend).
- Return to the supine position.
- Sit up and touch your toes to assume *paschimottasana*.
- Inhale and exhale.
- Lie down and lift your legs to do *Halasana* again.

Practise this ten times. All movements should be smooth and continuous.

OBESITY • 81

Supta Vajrasana

- Sit in *Vajrasana*.
- Arching the back, bend backwards and with the support of the arms put the corner of your head on the ground. Place your hands on your thighs.

- Breathe naturally and hold the posture for one and a half to two minutes (Count thirty to forty breaths).

The duration should be increased gradually.

Return to the starting position.

Ujjayi Pranayama

- Sit in *Padmasana* or *Sukhasana* with your hands on your knees in *Gyanmudra*. Fold back your tongue.
- Contract the throat and breathe deeply; it should produce a mild snoring sound.

Practise this twenty-seven times.

CHAPTER 8

Smoking

SMOKING

Enough has been said about the harm caused by tobacco consumption, but surprisingly a lot of youngsters continue to smoke. Their impressionable mind is easily influenced by tantalising advertisements and peer pressure, which makes them adopt the deadly habit. This suits the cigarette manufacturers, who according to investigations, target children younger than twelve years to ensure an increasing demand for their product. An American statistic shows that out of 400,000 people who die in the U.S. every year due to tobacco related ailments, ninety per cent started smoking during their childhood.

Almost all smokers intend not to smoke beyond five years, but they do not realise that it is an addiction that takes such a deep hold over their body that they are not able to give up the habit easily. Those with a stronger will do manage to quit, but with extreme difficulty. The worst part is that a smoker cannot escape the consequences of smoking even after he/she quits the habit. I know of an eighty year old gentleman who smoked from school and gave it up in his early thirties, but till today suffers from its consequences: wheezing, cough, breathlessness and weak lungs. Children should be made aware of the ill-effects of smoking so that they don't inculcate this vice, and if they do, will quit it without delay. There are several dangers related to smoking. These are:

i) Cancer: Tobacco smoke contains around 4000 chemicals out of which at least 400 are carcinogens and are responsible for most cancers of the mouth, larynx, pharynx and the lungs.

ii) **Heart Attack:** Cigarette smoke causes a hardening of the blood vessels and clumping of blood platelets. Both these conditions can lead to a heart attack.

iii) **Respiratory failure:** With tar from tobacco coating the lungs and smoke melting their tissues, these vital organs develop holes and lose their elasticity. At the same time, the cilia or hair in the respiratory tract get paralysed and cannot filter mucus and foreign matter entering the lungs. As a result, these substances accumulate in the lungs damaging them further and also attracting harmful microbes. Repeated lung infection is a common phenomenon in smokers and they can succumb to it.

iv) **Leukemia in progeny:** The children of smokers have a high risk of contracting leukemia.

Observing the existing trends, the World Bank has predicted that one out of two regular smokers will die of regular tobacco use and half of them will do so while still in their fifties.

Quitting an addiction may not be easy, but if a person is determined to do it and has made up his/her mind, the subconscious actively works on the conscious mind to support the decision and even the body stops craving for the poison. Yoga has

Smoking can cause leukemia in progeny

SMOKING • **87**

techniques to access the subconscious effectively. At the same time, yogic *asanas* and *Pranayama* strengthen the system while *Shatkarma* removes all harmful chemicals from the body.

A mixture of mint, jaggery (*gur*) and green chillies should be taken every day to absorb and eliminate the chemicals.

TECHNIQUE

Trikonasana III

- Stand with your feet apart and arms extended on the sides.

- Exhaling, bend forward.

- Holding your breath twist your trunk and touch your left foot with your right hand. Then, twisting to the other side, touch your right foot with your left hand.

- Return to the bent posture.

- Inhaling, return to the starting position.

Repeat the *asana* ten times.

Paschimottanasana

- Sit down with the legs extended in front.
- Inhaling, raise your arms.
- Exhaling, bend forward and try to hold the toes without bending your legs.
- Keep your head down.
- Breathe normally.
- Starting with five breaths, gradually increase the number to twenty.

Sarpasana

- Lie down on your stomach with your hands clasped behind.
- Inhaling, lift your head and chest while lifting up your arms.
- Hold the posture for as long as is comfortable.
- Exhaling, return to the starting position.

Repeat the *asana* ten times.

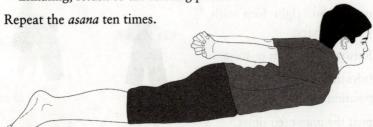

Ananda Madirasana

- Sit in *Vajrasana* and hold your ankles.
- Look up at the 'V' point.
- Take deep breaths and hold the position for as long as is comfortable.

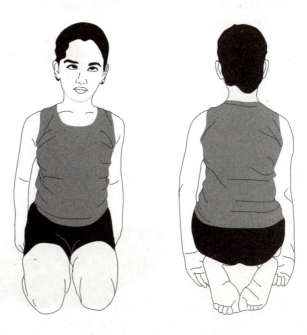

Kapalabhati Pranayama

- Sit in *Sukhasana* or *Padmasana* with your right hand on your face like in *Nadisodhana Pranayama*.
- Closing the right nostril, breathe out twenty times forcefully from the left. Inhalation should be natural.
- Closing the left nostril, do the same with the right nostril and then with both of them together.
- This is one round.

Practise three rounds.

SMOKING

Yoga mudra

- Sit in *Padmasana*.
- Keeping your hands behind you, hold your right wrist with your left hand.
- Take a deep breath
- Exhaling, bend forward and keep your forehead on the ground.
- Breathe normally for one minute.

Unmani Mudra

In this *Mudra*, one needs to take the mind to the various *charkas*. Hence it is necessary to familiarise oneself with their names and locations. The charka or energy centers are located on the spine in the following order:

　i)　Top of the head: *Sahasrara*
　ii)　Corner of the head: *Bindu*
　iii)　Behind the 'V' point: *Agya*
　iv)　Behind the throat: *Vishuddhi*
　v)　Behind the chest: *Anahata*
　vi)　Behind the navel: *Manipura*
　vii)　At the end of the spinal cord: *Swadhisthana*
　viii)　At the tip of the tail bone: *Mooladhara*

- Sit in *Padmasana*.
- Take a deep breath and concentrate on the *Bindu charka* for a few seconds.
- Start exhaling and closing the eyes while taking the attention down through each *charka*.

- By the time the mind reaches *Mooladhara*, the breath should be completely out and the eyes closed.

Practise the *Mudra* up to ten minutes, depending on the time available.

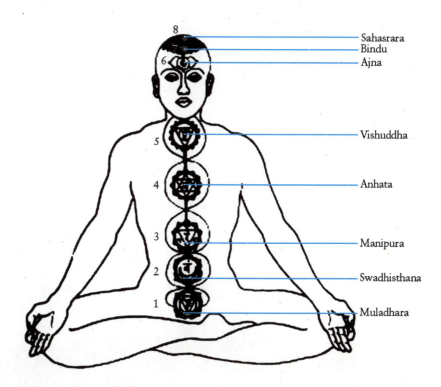

CHAPTER 9: Stress Ailments

STRESS AILMENTS

A friend's son was bed-wetting well into his teens, because of which he had become a complete recluse. The helpless parents did not know what to do as all therapies, conventional and alternative, had failed to give him any relief. That's when I happened to meet them and they mentioned their son's problem asking for any.help that yoga could provide. On my assurance that it could, they approached the harried boy who was now refusing to go to any more wonder therapists and some how managed to persuade him to give yoga a try. In the first week of his joining my class, the number of bed-wetting episodes came down from five or six to only three and in a year's time, he had been cured of the problem completely. Now, he is a successful professional with a wife and two children.

A traumatic experience in early childhood can cause acute stress on a young mind; the experience remains etched in the sub-conscience, adversely influencing the brain. Under stress, the brain's judgment is known to become erratic and its instructions to the body become faulty. This can lead to various problems, bedwetting being one of them. However, if the brain and nerves are made to relax and the negative influences diminished or eliminated, the problem disappears, and this is just what yoga does. Yogic meditation frees the mind and *Yoganidra* relaxes it. A regular exercise regimen also helps to strengthen the weakened nervous system.

Besides bedwetting and asthma, migraine and phobias are also psychosomatic problems common in children.

A migraine is an intense, gripping headache that generally begins on one side of the head, spreading gradually. Sometimes it can become severe in a matter of minutes and continue for days although the frequency of the attacks is not fixed. A migraine is sometimes accompanied by nausea and vomiting and usually preceded by a symptom called 'aura' which includes dizziness, numbness or bright flashes of light.

Migraines are usually treated with pain killers, which is not a permanent remedy. Six weeks of yoga on the other hand is known to cure the problem completely. *Suryanamaskar*, *Bhramari Pranayama* and *Kunjal* are the most effective for a migraine.

A phobia is a fear or an aversion to something. Experiencing intense fear in the face of grave peril is natural, but an adult petrified at the thought of sleeping alone in the dark, a la Tony Dorsett the football legend for instance, isn't. Dorsett admitted that he is Achluophobic and says that he believes in spirits walking around in complete darkness, a story he must have been told as a child. Indian film star Amitabh Bachchan too is scared of ghosts and could not sleep well after seeing the horror film *Bhoot*. He could not even bring himself to take a peep under his bed for fear of discovering a ghost there!

But fear of the unknown alone does not constitute phobia. A person can be phobic of a wide range of things such as birds, animals, insects, closed rooms, open spaces, height and so on. Even though these people

STRESS AILMENTS • 97

are aware that their fears are unfounded, they cannot do anything to prevent them. But yoga and meditation can change the situation and the treatment is more effective in childhood when the problem has not yet crystallised.

Stammering too is a psychosomatic disorder that affects the speech. Performing *Simhasana* however can help treat the problem.

TECHNIQUE

Naukasana

- Lie down on your back.
- Take a deep breath.
- Lift up your legs and trunk a foot above the ground with your arms extended before you. Your head, arms and feet should be at the same level.

- Hold the posture for as long as you can. Exhaling, return to the ground.
- Repeat the *asana* after a short rest.

Practise it five times.

Eka Pada Pranamasana

- Stand on your left leg with your hands folded in front and the right foot on the left thigh, just above the knee.
- Look straight ahead and breathe deeply twenty times.
- Now perform the *asana* with your right leg.

Natarajasana

- Stand straight.
- Lift the right leg and cross it over the left.
- Hold the right arm above the right leg with the hand hanging down.
- Hold the left hand in *gyan mudra* above the right wrist.
- Look straight ahead and breathe deeply twenty times.
- Repeat the same on the opposite side.

Chakrasana

- Lie down on your back.
- Bend your legs and place your feet next to your hips.
- Place your hands beside the neck with the fingers pointing towards your body.
- Lift first your pelvis, then the shoulders and lastly your head as high as possible, forming an arch.
- Breathe normally.
- Hold the posture for ten to twenty breaths.
- While returning to the initial position, first place your head on the ground, then the shoulders and last of all the hips.

Yogamudra Asana

- Sit in *Vajrasana*.
- Hold your right wrist with your left hand and exhaling, bend forward to keep your forehead on the ground.
- Breathe normally twenty times.
- Inhaling, return to the starting position.

Manduki Mudra

- Sit in *Vajrasana* and turn your feet out.
- Place your hands on your knees.
- Close your eyes and relax your body.
- Slowly open your eyes and gaze at the tip of your nose.
- Breathing slowly, hold the posture for as long as is comfortable.

Merudanda

- Sit on the floor with your feet placed in front.
- Hold the big toe on each foot and inhale.
- Balancing your weight on your hips, straighten your legs upward and side ways.
- Hold the posture for as long as you are comfortable.
- Return to the starting position and exhale.

Repeat the *asana* five times.

Bhramari Pranayama

- Sit in crossleg position.
- Plug both the ears with the index fingures.
- Close your eyes and take a deep breath.
- As you exhale utter mmmm.....

Repeat five times.

Kunjal

- Drink three to four glasses of warm, saline water on an empty stomach.
- Pressing your tongue with your fingers, try to regurgitate the water. It is best to bring out all of it, but if you can't don't worry, as contrary to popular belief, it causes no harm. The water will help to flush the intestines and the urinary tract.

Do not eat anything for at least half an hour after performing *Kunjal*.

CHAPTER 10

Urinary Tract & Digestive Tract Infections

URINARY TRACT & DIGESTIVE TRACT INFECTIONS

Urinary tract infection is a common ailment in children. It is caused when bacteria enter the bladder via the urethra taking hold of that organ. As a result, the urinary bladder gets inflamed leading to painful and too frequent urination and fetid urine. Sometimes the infection occurs without any symptoms. If it is not contained, it can travel to the kidney which is indicated by fever, vomiting and back pain, a condition which may need hospitalisation. If kidney infection is not eradicated, it can recur damaging this vital organ resulting in renal failure. Antibiotics are very effective in curing this infection, but they are harmful to the system and they do not take away from the danger of recurrent urinary tract infection. *Laghoo Shankha Prakshyalana*, a yogic *ghatkarma,* is extremely effective in preventing the infection from recurring.

Laghoo Shankha Prakshyalana is the most powerful *kriya* for food poisoning and gastroenteritis. Once, my son came home with severe cramps and diarrhea. His condition was so bad that he had visited the toilet three times in thirty minutes. As soon as I came to know of his condition, I heated some water and ignoring his protests, forced him to perform the *kriya*. His diarrhea was cured immediately.

TECHNIQUE

Laghoo Shankha Prakshyalana

- Heat six glasses of water.
- The water should be hot, but not so hot that you can't drink it quickly.
- Add two teaspoons of salt to it.

(Initially you can put only one teaspoon to see how your body reacts. You should have not more than two to three clear motions. Adjust the salt accordingly).

- Quickly drink two glasses of water and practise the following five *asanas* eight times each.

URINARY TRACT & DIGESTIVE TRACT INFECTIONS

Tadasana

- Stand with your feet together.
- Interlock your fingers and place your hands on your head.
- Inhaling, rise to your toes while stretching your arms above your head with the palms turned out and your face turned up.
- After stretching completely, quickly bring your heels down with a thud with your hands still on your head.

Repeat the *asana* eight times.

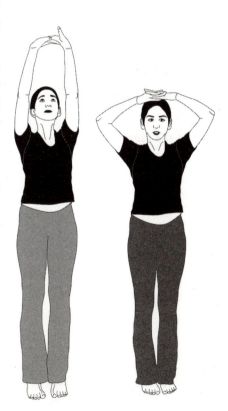

Triyaka Tadasana

- Stand with your feet apart.
- Interlock your fingers and stretch your arms above your head.
- Exhaling, bend to the left.
- Inhaling, straighten up.
- Practise the above on the other side.

Repeat the *asana* four times.

URINARY TRACT & •111
DIGESTIVE TRACT INFECTIONS

Katichakrasana

- Standing with your feet apart, extend your arms sideways.
- Twisting your waist, turn to the left while bringing the right hand to the left shoulder and the left hand to the right side of the waist from behind. Your palm should be turned out.
- Repeat the *asana* on your right side.

Practise the *asana* four times.

Triyak Bhujangasana

- Lie down on your stomach, with your hands on your sides.
- Inhaling, rise from the waist with your head held back, then turn your head to the left to look at your feet.
- Exhaling, return to the starting position.
- Repeat the *asana*, this time looking to your right.

Practise the *asana* four times.

URINARY TRACT & DIGESTIVE TRACT INFECTIONS

Udarakarshanasana

- Squat on the floor with your hands on your knees.
- Turn your body to the left keeping the right knee near the left foot. Your head should be turned too.
- Return to the starting position.
- Repeat on the other side.

Practise four such rounds.

Now drink two more glasses of the saline water and practice the *asanas* again.

After repeating the whole process, visit the toilet to evacuate the bowels. If you do not feel the urge, wait for a while but do not sit down, just keep walking. One generally has a clear motion after this *kriya*. Some may have two or three loose motions and those who suffer from constipation may not have a good motion the first time. Adjusting the amount of salt however rectifies the condition; a high saline level can enhance the *kriya's* effect while a low saline level can decrease it. But do not use more than two and a half teaspoons of salt.

Very young children should not be made to perform this *kriya*. It is ideal for children above the age of fourteen or fifteen, but twelve or thirteen year olds can do it if necessary.

CHAPTER 11

Meditation

MEDITATION

Childhood trauma is not the only source of stress in schoolchildren. Parental pressure, setting of unrealistic targets, intense competition, exam tension and the fear of failure also add to their already burdened minds. Apart from falling prey to various ailments, their behaviour can be extremely disturbing. We've all heard and read about schoolchildren committing suicide; some have even taken the drastic step of shooting their own classmates. Since stress is inevitable, children need to be taught to release it in a positive way so as to protect their mind and body from harm.

Meditation is an age-old method to get rid of stress. During this practice, the rate at which the heart beats drops, respiration is slowed down and even the brain functions at a lower pace—all signs of a highly relaxed body and mind. Lactic acid, a stress-related hormone which is generally expelled from the body during sleep, is eliminated four times faster during meditation. Not only does meditation de-stress the system, it also sharpens the intellect.

Here's an interesting tale that proves my point. There was once a brilliant princess who could not settle on a suitor because she found no man who could match her in wits. She would scorn them all and send them away. The king, her father, was enraged by his daughter's arrogance and as a punishment, ordered his men to bring before him the most dim-witted man in his kingdom to be his daughter's spouse. The king's men searched high and low till they finally chanced upon a man who was cutting the tree-branch he was sitting on. 'Who can be more foolish than him?' they thought and brought the man to the king who solemnised the marriage according to plan, much to the chagrin of the princess. The angry bride gave vent to her anger by showering her husband with abuses. Unable to bear her derision, the husband left their home and went into the jungle, determined to improve his lot in life. He prayed to Goddess Saraswati seeking Divine intervention. Eventually, his prayers were answered and the Goddess of Learning blessed him with knowledge and intellect, helping him become a great scholar. He wrote great volumes of poetry and epics and came to be known as the poet Kalidasa. His works *Kumara Sambhava*, *Meghdoot* and *Abhigyanam Shakuntalam* are highly revered texts.

Kalidasa's intense prayers to Saraswati were nothing but meditation. Intense concentration on anything, be it an object's symbol, a sound or a deity, is called meditation. But focusing the mind on one object alone is not possible for most people, especially children. There are however various kinds of meditation to suit individual age, temperaments and capacity.

The following is a form of meditation for clearing the psyche, which children can practice easily.

MEDITATION • 117

TECHNIQUE

- Sit straight in *Padmasana* or *Sukhasana*.
- Listen to and identify the sounds you can hear; first the louder ones for a minute or two and then the less audible ones for another minute. Finally, try to discern the faintest of sounds you can hear for yet another minute.

- Then try to hear the sound of your breath for a minute.
- Now imagine your breath has turned red. (Children with a temper should imagine pink instead).
- Count the red breath twenty times.
- After twenty breaths, imagine it changing its colour to become orange.
- Again count twenty breaths.
- Then comes the colour yellow.
- In this way, imagine your breath in all the colours of the rainbow.
- If a child is unable to visualise colour, he or she can just repeat mentally the name of the colour and count the breaths such as, 'I am breathing the colour red, one.' 'I am breathing the colour red, two'.

Ideally the counting should be done backwards from twenty to one.

- After VIBGYOR has been exhausted, move to white or gold.

(If the child dislikes colours or feels restless and uncomfortable, the practice should be discontinued and some other form of meditation should be tried. I have enumerated several meditation techniques in my book *Yoga and Meditation for All Ages*).

- Thereafter, the child should be made aware of the space or screen (called *Chidakasha*) before his closed eyes and should take note of

MEDITATION • 119

everything that appears and disappears from there. It is said that past impressions manifest themselves on this screen as forms, figures, objects and colours because that is how the brain stores them. They surface during meditation and when confronted by the conscious mind, they start losing their strength.

- After four to five minutes of observing the screen, or when the child starts feeling restless, he or she should chant *Om* seven, eleven or twenty-seven times. This is done by taking a deep breath and exhaling through the mouth while saying 'Oo…' half the way, then 'Uu…' for a short period and finally 'Mm…' till all the breath is out.

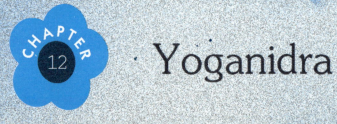

CHAPTER 12

Yoganidra

YOGANIDRA

Famous men like Henry Ford, Thomas Edison and many renowned artists and writers achieved greatness with the power of their own subconscious mind. It may seem strange that with such great power within us we still suffer, but that's because the subconscious mind does not work independently. It derives its conclusion on the basis of information provided by the conscious mind in the form of spoken words, thoughts and experiences. Once the subconscious mind has decided on the course of action, nobody and nothing can stop it from accomplishing that object.

The subconscious mind can be made to work for us by providing it with the right information at the right time. It has been seen that this mind is alert and receptive when the conscious mind has stopped its restless activities and is relaxed—a state indicated by alpha brain waves.

The brain generates electricity in the form of brain waves which are named according to their frequencies. Beta, the fastest waves, dominate the working hours when the conscious mind is active: thinking, worrying, planning and calculating. During deep sleep delta, the slowest waves, are emitted. The other two waves, alpha and theta, are produced depending on the state of relaxation, theta being the slower ones. Though the brain is more relaxed when lower frequency waves are being emitted, it is the alpha waves that are the most beneficial. Not only is the body better restored in this condition, but the subconscious mind can also be accessed in this state.

Alpha waves are naturally produced during sleep and immediately before and after it. Although the period of their emission is too short to be taken advantage of, those people in whom this period is longer have amazing insight. Mozart was said to get his inspirations in this surreal state.

Yoganidra is a practice that systematically relaxes the body and mind resulting in the production of alpha waves. This technique was developed by my guru Paramahamsa Swami Sri Satyananda Saraswati on the basis of two interesting personal experiences. The first one occurred transporting him to a dreamlike state whenever he performed *nyasa*, a *tantrik* yogic worship ritual that involves touching the various body parts in a particular sequence.

The second experience occurred during his days as a student. Whenever he was sent off to mind a class in the absence of its teacher, he would doze off while the students continued with their recitation of mantras. During the passing out ceremony of that school where my guru*ji* was also invited, the boys started reciting verses which to guru*ji*'s great surprise he knew verbatim even though he had never studied them. He then realised that he had indeed heard them while he was dozing. He then used the principle of *nyasa* to attain a dream like state and called it *Yoganidra*.

There are various self-hypnosis methods to access the subconscious mind, but *Yoganidra* is perhaps the most scientific of them all as it

relaxes the body following the exact sequence as mapped in the brain. When the body is completely relaxed, a suggestion to the effect of achieving a goal is made. The goal can be a short-term one such as giving up smoking or a long-term one such as becoming the best footballer in the world or even a general one like becoming a more positive person.

Yoganidra can also be used to memorise lessons. My guru*ji* taught various scriptures and languages, including some foreign ones, to his prime disciple. The young disciple who had never received any formal education mastered them all in an amazingly short time thanks to *Yoganidra*.

Yoganidra should be said in a soft and lilting tone. The place where it is practiced should be comfortable and semi-dark. The following text can be recorded and played for convenience.

TECHNIQUE

Yoganidra

- 'Lie down in *Shavasana* and make yourself comfortable (*long pause*).
- Feel your breath in the nostrils (*long pause*).
- Breathe deeply and say the following in your mind, "I am breathing

in, twelve", "I am breathing out, twelve". "I am breathing in, eleven", "I am breathing out, eleven".

- Go on till you reach one and again feel your breath in the nostrils for a minute or two. (*Wait till the counting is over*).
- Now mentally repeat after me the words I say, then think of that body part and tell it to relax. For example if I say right hand thumb, you take your mind to your right hand thumb and say these in your mind, "Right hand thumb relax".
- Right hand thumb (*pause*), index finger (*pause*), middle finger – ring finger – little finger – right arm – right shoulder – right hip – right thigh – right calf – foot – big toe – second toe – third toe – fourth toe and fifth toe.

(*Repeat on the left side*).

- The back – the head – forehead – the eyes – the nose – the mouth – the jaw – chest – stomach – and abdomen.

(For better relaxation repeat it once or even twice).

- Repeat your resolution three times in your mind.

(The resolution must be decided and framed in advance. It should be a short sentence with only positive words. For example instead of saying "I will not smoke", say "I am giving up smoking".)

- Feel your body, move it a little, then slowly stretch and open your eyes.'

CHAPTER 13

Health Facts

HEALTH FACTS

Health, like everything else in this world, is governed by the principle of cause and effect. When a mango tree is planted, it will yield mangoes, not cherries. If one does not eat iron, one will be anaemic; if a woman does not take adequate calcium, her bones will be porous and if a baby does not take in enough protein, its growth will be stunted. To avoid these unpleasant and often irreversible consequences, it is essential that children follow certain health rules.

Right Food

Yoga refers to the human body as *annamaya shareera* meaning 'a body of food'. Only the right food can help build a healthy body, hence nutritional deficiencies should not be allowed to occur. In children, deficiencies can hamper physical as well as mental growth. At the same time, synthetic supplements should be avoided. The body has its own natural mechanism to deal with food which should not be interfered with. Nature supplies all the required nutrients in fruits and vegetables. One only needs to know what to eat.

A good digestive system helps in the proper utilisation of food. Children generally possess such a system and the endeavour must be to keep it such by ensuring that the intestines are clean. Castor oil taken once a week at bedtime is the traditional way of ensuring good digestion. Harmful microbes often enter the digestive tract creating a toxic

Spinach increases uric acid

128 • YOGA FOR SCHOOL CHILDREN

atmosphere. They can be destroyed by taking turmeric and margosa. Children should be administered these two items frequently. Turmeric is especially good because of its various health promoting qualities; it is antiseptic, antibacterial, anti-fungal, anti-inflammatory, anti-rheumatism and anti-cancerous. Bitter gourd and honey are also good; the former helps in good digestion and the latter keeps the intestines sterile.

A healthy immune system can ward off all infections. Such a system needs Vitamins A and C to function properly. Indian gooseberry (*amla*) is not only one of the richest sources of Vitamin C, but is also considered highly therapeutic in Ayurveda. It is said that a person who takes *amla, haldi* (turmeric) and honey regularly will never fall prey to any infection. *Amla* with almond is said to keep one's eyesight intact. Serious eye ailments such as glaucoma and cataract are also supposed to be prevented by their consumption.

Environmental pollutants are a great threat to one's general health. Mint and jaggery (*gur*) are believed to absorb and eliminate all harmful elements from the body.

Contrary to certain theories, milk is considered extremely beneficial in Ayurveda. Not only is it a complete food in itself that can prevent nutritional deficiencies, except those caused by a lack of Vitamin C, but it also soothes and protects the intestinal wall

Amla with almond preserves eyesight

from its acidic contents. Milk products are also good for health. Curd contains plenty lot of lactobacillus, the friendly bacteria that can kill all harmful bacteria in the intestine. Cow's milk is preferred to buffalo milk as it has a lower fat content and possesses therapeutic qualities too.

Salad is good for health but due to the use of chemical fertilisers, pesticides, germicides and preservatives, the body may absorb and retain some harmful chemicals. Further more, tapeworms have now been discovered to harm vegetarians who get the parasite from raw vegetables grown in contaminated soil. To be on the safer side, only vegetables with a thick skin should be eaten raw. For example cucumber. Leafy and underground vegetables are thought to carry tapeworm eggs.

Leafy vegetables should be washed thoroughly before being cooked. They not only provide bulk to the food helping better evacuation, but also absorb fat from the intestines. The use of spinach should be minimised as it is rich in purine bodies that increase uric acid in the system which can lead to arthritis, gout and renal problems.

Too much acidic food should also be avoided as they are believed to speed the ageing process. Alkaline foods neutralise the stomach acids and help maintain a perfect pH balance, a must to remain healthy. It is also seen that cancer cells die within hours when kept in an alkaline solution. Finally, following the golden rule of eating only when one is hungry and never over-eating has its advantages.

Right Breathing

Adequate intake of oxygen is essential for good health and a lack of it leads to poor blood quality that fails to revitalise the body cells. As a result, neither the brain nor the body will function to their optimum capacity. With trillions of cells demanding oxygen every single second, one needs to take plenty of air to the lungs. Yogic breathing is the ideal way to achieve that. It should first be learnt in *Shavasana* and later in any position. If a child makes a conscious effort to breathe like that most of the time, it slowly becomes a habit and he will always breathe deeply, even as an adult.

TECHNQUE

- Lie down in *Shavasana*.
- Breathe to raise the abdomen first.
- Then breathe to expand the chest.
- Finally breathe to lift your shoulders.

- To exhale, first release air from the upper part of the lungs and then the lower.
- Exhale till the abdomen is squeezed to the fullest.

Yogic breathing not only ensures perfect oxygenation of the system, it also exercises the lungs and the diaphragm rendering them super healthy.

The diaphragm lies in the abdominal cavity separating it from the chest cavity. Its continuous movement makes respiration possible. Its downward movement creates a vacuum in the chest that draws the outside air into the lungs, while its upward movement compresses the lungs squeezing the stale, used air out.

Right Posture

A straight spine is extremely important for good health. The spinal cord which carries messages to and from the brain passes through the spine and any pressure on it can lead to dissipation of the nerves' current, disturbing a body's functions.

Furthermore, according to yoga the *ida nadi* and *pirgala nadi,* the subtle energy channels that distribute mental and physical energies respectively to all body parts, are also located in the spine and a bad posture can disturb their flow causing low energy, diseases and impaired mental faculties.

Right Attitude

Children should cultivate a positive attitude as that alone leads to happiness. Good health goes hand in hand with a happy mind. Happiness does not depend on one's achievements. A research team of the University of California, Riverside, led by Professor Sonja Lyubomirsky found happiness as the key to success and not the other way round. Many other studies too have revealed that having a sunny outlook appeared to precede good fortune. Psychologists say that happiness makes people more sociable, generous and more productive at work so that they make more money.

Children who practice yoga and meditation and follow the above mentioned health rules have the best chance of being healthy, happy and successful and enjoy life better.

Some rules to be observed while performing yogic *asanas*:

i) All yogic practices mentioned in this book should be performed on an empty stomach, that is either in the morning before breakfast, or two hours after a light meal and three hours after a heavy meal.

ii) *Asanas* should be practiced on a firm and comfortable surface; the bare floor is too hard and a mattress or a spongy mat too soft. A folded blanket is ideal.

iii) Cotton clothes should be worn while performing the *asanas* so that the skin can breathe easily.

HEALTH FACTS •133

iv) There should not be any pressure on the body as that can disturb the subtle pranic flow. Therefore, your clothes and wrist watch should be loosely tied.

v) The yogic routine should commence with *Suryanamaskara*.

vi) *Shavasana* should be performed after each major *asana* and at the end of all the *asanas*, before the *pranayamas*.

vii) When introducing a new *asana*, only one or two rounds of that *asana* should be performed and the number of rounds should be gradually increased. Similarly, for static *asanas*, in the beginning they should be held only for a few seconds.

viii) *Pranayamas* should be practiced after all the *asanas*. *Nadisodhana Pranayama* is the first one.

ix) Meditation should be done at a fixed time every day.

x) *Yoganidra* can be done anytime, but practiced at bedtime it induces sound sleep leading to better repair of the body's faults.

xi) Food should be taken only ten to fifteen minutes after performing the *asanas* and *pranayama*.

xii) Children with serious health problems (especially of the heart and brain) should not practise the yoga mentioned in this book, but consult a competent yoga therapist.

xiii) Children with minor health problems can practise all the given *asanas*, but only after seeking the consent of their physician.

Success follows happiness

Index

Ananda Madirasana	89
Bhastrika Pranayama	43
Bhoochari Mudra	30
Bhramari Pranayama	104
Breathing Technique	130
Chakki Chalana	60
Chakrasana	100
Cycling	63
Dhanurasana	22, 59, 78
Dritahalasana	80
Dwikonasana	48
Eka Pada Pranamasana	98
Halasana	23
Hasta Utthanasana	36
Hasta Uttahanasana II	37
Kandhrasana	57
Kapalabhati Pranayama	90
Katichakrasana	111
Kunjal	105
Laghoo Shankha Prakshyalana	108
Leg Pressing	64
Leg Rotation	62
Lolasana	41
Makarasana	42
Manduki Mudra	102
Marjari Asana	56
Matsyasana	40
Meditation	117
Merudanda	103
Moola Bandha	66
Nadisodhan Pranayama	24
Naukasana	97
Naukasanchalana	61
Natarajasana	99

Neti	50
Paschimottanasana	31, 88
Pranamasana	21
Sambhavi Mudra	30
Sarpasana	88
Sarvangasana	39, 58
Shankukhi Mudra	49
Shashankabhujangasana	75, 76, 77
Shashankasana	29
Shatkarma	67
Simhasana	47
Supta Vajrasana	81
Suryanamaskar	17
Tadagi Mudra	65
Tadasana	109
Triyak Bhujangasana	112
Triyaka Tadasana	110
Trikonasana I	73
Trikonasana II	74
Trikonasana III	87
Udarakarshanasana	113
Ujjayi Pranayama	82
Unmani Mudra	92
Ushtrasana	38
Vipareet Karani Mudra	79
Yogamudra Asana	101
Yoganidra	123
Yoga mudra	91